THE FUNNY GUY

JONATHAN W.MAUPIN

Order this book online at www.trafford.com
or email orders@trafford.com

Most Trafford titles are also available at major online book retailers.

Printed in the United States of America.

ISBN: 978-1-4669-2037-8 (sc)
ISBN: 978-1-4669-2036-1 (e)

Trafford rev. 03/27/2012

www.trafford.com

North America & International
toll-free: 1 888 232 4444 (USA & Canada)
phone: 250 383 6864 • fax: 812 355 4082

In a world where frustration and sadness seem to be the norm, The Funny Guy breaks the mold. The comic strip focuses on a young man and his everyday situations, which become comical. The cartoon's main character (Fun) is a modern-day Charlie Chaplin! His days begin normal and end hilarious! And the people he interacts with each day represent every walk of life. From a pushy landlord, a quick-to-write-a-ticket traffic cop, and a slang-talking hobo. The Funny Guy is a cartoon in which every person--no matter what race, age, or religion--can appreciate and enjoy.

John W. Maupin
12/11/00

PAY YOUR RENT

LETS SEE WHAT WE HAVE HERE! JUNK MAIL, JUNK MAIL, BILL! JUNK MAIL, JUNK MAIL, I'M NOT PAYING THAT!!
MR. FUN

I NEVER GET ANYTHING GOOD IN THE MAIL! HEY, WHATS THIS ON MY DOOR?

APT 11

YOU
HAVE
30 DAYS
TO
VACATE!

MAN OL MAN!!
I FORGOT TO
PAY MY
RENT!!

CARDBOARD

HEY FUN, HOW ARE YA?
OH GREAT, HERE COMES "BUSTER", MY LANDLORD!!

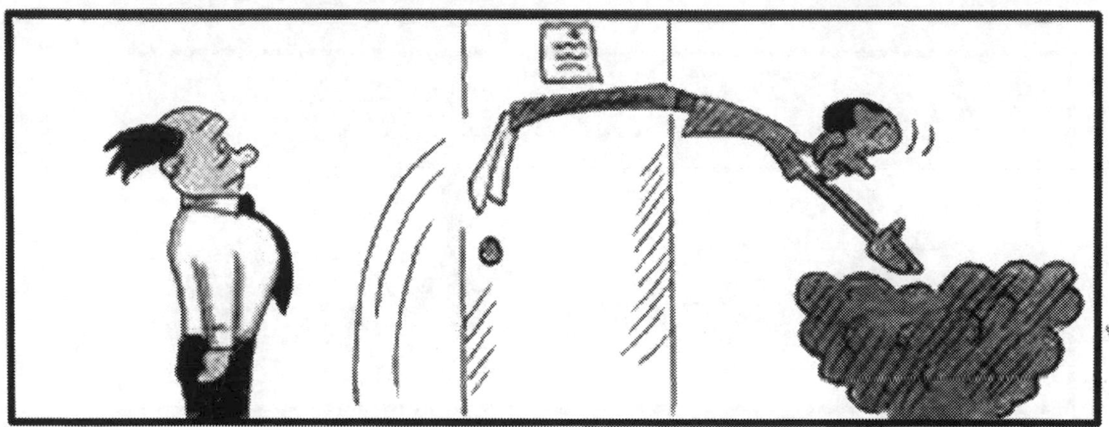

WHATS WRONG WITH YOU??

OH, THATS NOT FOR you.

I PUT IT ON THE WRONG DOOR. BUT IF YOU DONT PAY YOUR RENT TODAY, ILL MAKE ONE FOR YOU!

WHEW!! THAT WAS A CLOSE ONE!!

THAT'S WAY TOO MUCH!

HOTDOG
CHARCOAL
MATCHES

LIGHTER
FLUID

LIGHTER
FLUID
PLOOP!

MATCH

POOF!

BETTER WATCH YOURSELF

RUFF!!
RUFF!!
RUFF!!
RUFF!!
GRRRRRR
RUFF RUFF
RUFF
RUFF
HMMMM
RUFF RUFF RUFF
RUFF

RUFF
RUFF RUFF
RUFF

RUFF RUFF RUFF
EHHH

RUFF
RUFF RUFF

HA HA HA HA HA HA
GRRRRR

GRRRRR

SNAP!!

DO THE
RIGHT
THING

Pssss!

HEY, COME HERE KID.

WHERE YA BEEN ??

WELL I'VE BEEN TRYING MY BEST TO AVOID YOU!

AVOID ME?? WHY?? I ENJOY LISTENING TO YOU COMPLAIN, I MEAN TALK!!

EHH, YOU DON'T HAVE TO LISTEN TO ME.

AWW COME ON KID, I KNOW YA GOT SOME GOOD OL JUICEY PROBLEMS TO COMPLAIN ABOUT..

I DONT HAVE TO TALK TO YOU BOUT MY PROBLEMS..

..I CAN TALK TO THE MAN UPSTAIR!
DIDNT GET HIM THIS TIME, BUT THEIRS ALWAYS NEXT TIME!

IT'LL BE OK

EVERYDAY IT'S THE SAME OL ROUTINE, WORK 8 HOURS...

PUNCH OUT...
CLICK!

WALK HOME FROM WORK, THEN START THIS PROCESS ALL OVER AGAIN TOMORROW.

WHEN WILL I SEE SOME CHANGE??!

WHY IS IT SO IMPORTANT FOR YOU TO SEE CHANGE?

RIGHT NOW, I CAN'T SEE ANYTHING.

CHANGE STARTS INSIDE YOU, NOT OUTSIDE.

But sir, I'm OK
inside my body,
It's the things
around me that
I wanna see
changed!!

CHANGE YOUR THINKING..

UHH...HELLO? ARE YOU STILL THERE? OH WELL, GUESS I'LL GO HOME.

I'M ALWAYS WITH YOU.

THE BOMB

AHH, THIS guys, CHEATING AGAIN!
I DONT CHEAT, THATS CALLED PLAYING SMART.
SAME THING RED.

KNOCK KNOCK KNOCK

EHH, I CAN'T WIN AT THIS GAME.

KNOCK KNOCK KNOCK

I Think you BETTER get The DOOR FUN.
WHY ME?
CAUSE ITS your PLACE.

I GOTTA DO EVERYTHING

TICK
TICK
TICK

TICK
TICK
TICK

WHAT IS THIS.
TICK
TICK
TICK
TICK
TICK
TICK
TICK

TICK
TICK
TICK

EEK!!!

YO FELLAS, ITS A BOMb!!

TICK TICK TICK TICK
TICK
TICK
TICK
TICK

LISTEN guys, WE JUST NEED TO STAY CALM.

TICK TICK TICK
TICK
TICK
TICK
TICK

I THINK ONE OF US NEEDS TO TAKE IT OUTSIDE.

YOU TAKE IT!!
NO YOU TAKE IT!!
HEY, I DON'T WANT IT!
TICK
TICK
TICK
TICK
TICK
TICK
TICK
TICK

KNOCK
KNOCK
KNOCK

WHO COULD THAT be?! DONT THEY Know WE'RE busy?

EXCUSE ME SIR, BUT I DELIVERED A box HERE by MISTAKE.

IT'S A CLOCK...

A CLOCK.. CLOSE CALL!!
CAN WE FINISH OUR GAME NOW??

KNOCK! KNOCK! KNOCK!
AN HOUR LATER...
DO YOU GUYS HEAR A KNOCKING SOUND?
NOT ME!
ME NIETHER

STRANGE
DOG

HMMM... LETS SEE WHATS IN THE PAPER TODAY.
DAILY NEWS

DOG NEEDS A HOME

Oh boy, I'VE ALWAYS WANTED A DOG! I'M gONNA DO This.
DAILY NEWS

Hope you Enjoy him!
Thanks!

Whats the DEAL with that Goofy Bowtie you're WEARING??

WERE gonna have sooo Much FUN!

5 MINUTES LATER..

HERE YA go boy, GOOD TASTING Dog FOOD!

ALRighty, HAVE AT IT boy!

SNIFF
SNIFF
SNIFF

WHAT THE?!?

TOLD YA This Dog WAS STRANGE!
Toothpick
EMPTY CANS OF CAVIAR
CAVIAR

LISTEN, I CANT KEEP THIS DOG, HE'S TOO HIGH MAINTENCE.
NO PROBLEM. WE'LL TAKE HIM BACK.

EH, THAT DOG WAS PROBABLY OWNED BY SOME RICH GUY!!

VROOM!
?
PET WORLD

SLOW DOWN THOMAS. THIS IS THE PLACE. I SURE HOPE POOPSIES OK. I CAN'T WAIT TO SEE HIM. I'M GONNA BUY HIM THE BIGGIEST MILK BONE THERE IS!!

THIS COULDN'T BE, IT'S TO COINCIDENTAL!
I HOPE THEY DIDN'T TOUCH HIS BOWTIE, CAUSE I SPENT ALOT OF MONEY FOR IT!
YEP, HE'S THE OWNER.

NO GAMES,
PLEASE

GOSH! I'VE gotta find A MEAL. I'M sooooo Hungry!

OK! OK! SHUT up ALREADY!
GROWL

HOSPITAL
HMMMM..

Thats it! There should be lots of food in this place!

OUT of THE WAY! WE'VE got A SICK MAN HERE!!
OOOH

Boy, oH Boy! HERE I COME FOOD!!

THE DOCTOR WILL BE IN TO SEE YOU SOON.

COULD YOU TELL HIM TO BRING ME A SANDWICH?

WELL MR. FUN, your X-RAYS don't show ANYTHING.
Munch Munch Munch Munch

HEY doc? COULD I HAVE ANOTHER MILKSHAKE?
Uhh... SURE.

AHHH!! This is The Life! Food whenever you WANT! Who CAN beat THAT?!

THE NEXT DAY
MR. FUN, YOU'RE A HEALTHY MAN! YOU'RE FREE TO go!!
Spaghetti

GO? Why?

BYE!!
MUNCH
CRUNCH CRUNCH CRUNCH
CHIPS

I THINK I ATE TO MUCH.
BURP!
CHIPS
GROWL!

I KNOW I ATE TOO MUCH!
OOOOH!!
GROWL!!

FORGET THIS, I'M going BACK TO THAT hospital!
GROWL

A GREAT SACRIFICE

$15.00

OK, LETS SEE IF I HAVE ENOUGH TO BUY THAT TURKEY.

FIVE, TEN, FIFTEEN.. JUST ENOUGH!

STORE

JOEY?! I'M SORRY HONEY, but I ONLY HAD ENOUGH TO PAY THE bills. I HAVE NO MONEY FOR A TURKEY!

AWW MAN! NO TURKEY?? Its NOT THE SAME WITHOUT TURKEY!

POOR LITTLE FELLOW.

Ehh, THEY'LL BE ALRIGHT!!

COME ON JOEY, WE'LL FIND SOMETHING TO EAT.

WAAHH!
?

HERE KID, I WANT YOU AND YOUR MOM TO HAVE THIS! HAPPY THANKSGIVING!!

THANKS MISTER!

WOW,
I FEEL
gREAT!
IM gLAD
I DID THAT!

NOW
MY
STOMACh,
THATS A
DIFFERENT
STORY.
GRRRR!

LETSSEE, DO
I HAVE
ENOUgh TO
buy ANOTHER
TURKEY....
Nope, Ehh.
HEY MISTER,
HOLD up!!

My MOM
AND I
WANT you
TO SPEND
ThANKSgiving
OVER OUR
HOUSE.
WILL
YA??
SURE
KID.

I'M SURE
gLAD I
CAUghT up
WITh you
MISTER.
So is MY
STOMACh!

A LOST BALLOON

SWIFF!!!

WHAAAH!

WHATS WRONG KID??
My balloons stuck.

DON'T WORRY KID, I'LL TAKE CARE OF IT.

It's up THERE!
GEEZ!!

WHAT DID I GET MYSELF INTO.
DONT LOOK DOWN,
SWIFF!!!

OH GREAT!
POWERLINES
GOT IT!!
POP!
WHATS That NOISE?
OUCH!

HERE goes your BALLOON.

MA, MA, MY BALLOON!! WHAAAAH!!
EH, you'LL GET OVER IT KID.

QUIT WORRYING

BLUE

HEY FUN, THE BOSS WANTS TO SEE YOU UP STAIRS, IN HIS OFFICE!!
BLUE

P
ME?? WHY ME??

HMMM.. MAYBE HE WANTS TO GIVE ME A PAY RAISE.
MAYBE I'M GETTING FIRED.
WOW!! THATS A LONG WAY DOWN!!

ALL THIS THINKING IS DRIVING ME NUTS!
MR. MANN C.E.O PAINT-INC.
AWW MAN. I JUST KNOW IT'S GONNA BE BAD..
KNOCK!
KNOCK!
KNOCK!
COME IN.

You wanted to see me Boss!?
No...

Well, one of the guys told me you requested to see me.
I asked to see Mr. Finch...

And unless you've change your name to "Finch", Mr. Fun, you're free to go.

EHH, I KNEW THERE WAS NOTHING TO WORRY ABOUT!
MR. MANN C.E.O PAINT, INC.
SLAM!

BORED?

YOU'RE BORED, HUH?!

I'VE GOT AN IDEA FOR YOU PAL!

OK, OK! SO DOING LAUNDRY WASN'T SUCH A GREAT IDEA.
DETERGENT

OK THEN, TRY THIS.
CHECKERS ARENT SO MUCH FUN WITHOUT A PARTENER, HUH?

WELL, WHAT ABOUT..
POP!

OOOH, you've got your OWN IDEA!

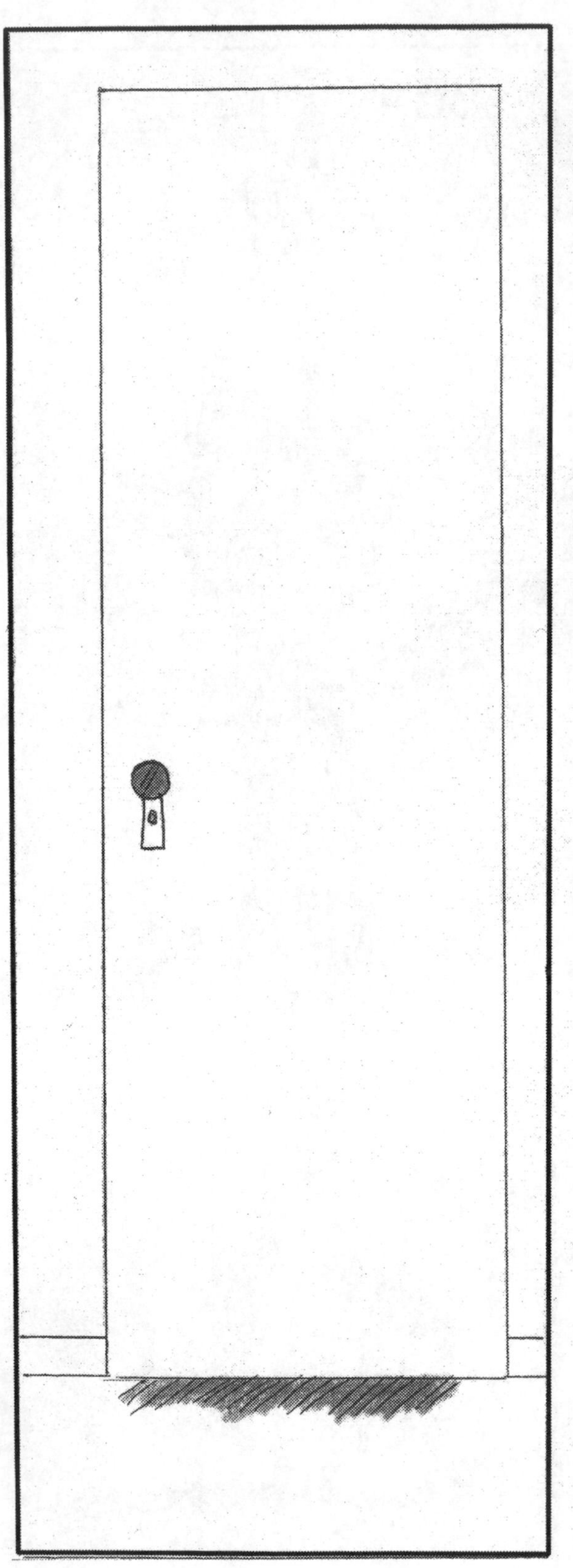

IT'S RAINING! WASN'T THAT GOOD OF AN IDEA EITHER.
OH SHUT UP!!

STOP TALKING TO YOURSELF

MIRROR SHOP

THANKS MR. BOB, SEE YA NEXT TIME!
$10.00

HEY BUDDY! NICE TO SEE YOU AGAIN! LONG-TIME NO TALK!

LISTEN, I DIDN'T PURCHASE THIS MIRROR SO I COULD HAVE A CONVERSATION WITH MY REFLECTION!
$10.00

WELL, TECHNICALLY ONE WOULD CONSIDER THIS A CONVERSATION!

THATS IT!!
IVE HEARD
ENOUGH!
BANANA PILL

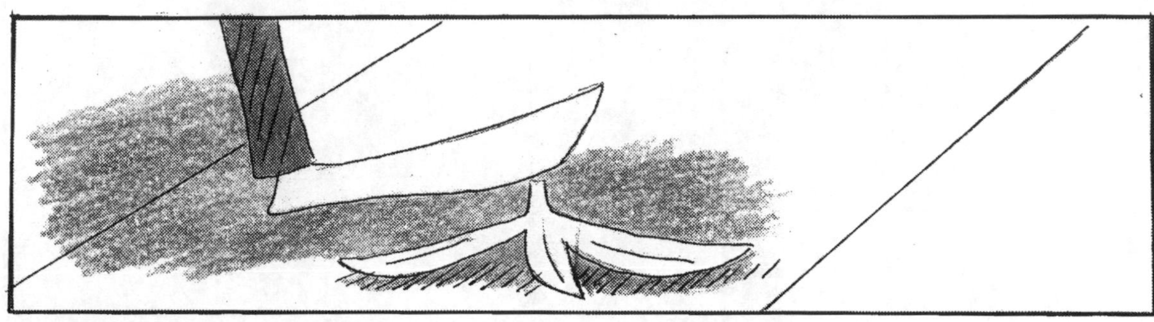

WHOOPS!
SMASH!!

HEY GUY!?! I
THINK THAT STORE
HAS A NO RETURN
POLICY!!

ALL THAT WORK FOR NOTHING!!

B.C
BEFORE
CARTOONS
WHEEL

SNAP!!!

TICK TICK TICK
LATER THAT DAY...

Z Z Z Z Z Z Z Z Z Z Z Z Z
NIGHT TIME...

MORNING TIME...

EEEEK!
SMASH!
BOOM

BOOM! BOOM!
UGH!
BOOM!

BRA
THE FUNNY GUY
Z Z Z
Z Z Z
Z Z
TM LAUGH-ALOT-PRODUCTIONS©
John W. Maupin

THE END